W9-AEP-120

DOWN HOME AT MISS DESSA'S

written by Bettye Stroud
illustrated by Felicia Marshall

LEE & LOW BOOKS Inc. • New York

For Howard, who has always shared my dreams
—B.S.

In loving dedication to my father Melvin and mother
Darlene, the two wonderful people who continued to
believe in me when I found it so hard to believe in myself
—F.M.

LEE & LOW BOOKS Inc., 95 Madison Avenue, New York, NY 10016

Printed in Hong Kong by South China Printing Co. (1988) Ltd.

Book Design by Tania Garcia
Book Production by Our House

The text is set in 14 point Garamond
The illustrations are rendered in an acrylic and acrylic gloss medium on watercolor paper.

The editors gratefully acknowledge the resource provided by *Step It Down* by Bessie Jones
and Bess Lomax Hawes (published by The University of Georgia Press),
which includes a description of the traditional game of "Zudie-O."

10 9 8 7 6 5 4 3 2 1
First Edition

Library of Congress Cataloging-in-Publication Data
Stroud, Bettye
Down home at Miss Dessa's/by Bettye Stroud;
illustrated by Felicia Marshall.—1st ed.
p.   cm.
Summary: In the South, in the 1940s, two young
Afro-American sisters spend the day caring for an elderly neighbor.
ISBN 1-880000-39-3
[1. Sisters—Fiction. 2. Neighborliness—Fiction. 3. Afro-Americans—Fiction.
4. Old age—Fiction.] I. Marshall, Felicia, ill. II. Title.
PZ7.S92473Do 1996
[Fic]—dc20   96-33846
CIP AC

Author's Note

Along the country dirt roads of the South in the late 1940s, farmhouses were often few and far between. As a result, supportive, caring neighbors were all-important. Neighbors formed a vital part of the network and fabric that united and held together the African American community. They provided aid when needed and, sometimes, simply offered companionship.

The elderly were then, and are still today much more likely to be alone. My "Miss Dessa" is the epitome of the elderly who have much love, knowledge, and experience to share. My childhood with such wonderful people as these contributed greatly to who I am today.

Perhaps this book can serve as evidence of the joy brought into the lives of young and old alike when generations come together to love, to share, and to protect.

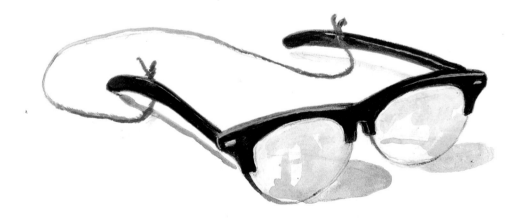

Miss Dessa was an old woman when we met her and her house was even older. She lived at the end of our dirt road and kept an eye on us— mending each skinned knee or bruised elbow we came crying about. Miss Dessa always knew how to make us feel better.

"Why do her glasses always hang on the end of her nose?" Baby Sister whispered. Baby Sister thought those glasses would fall right off and break one day.

One morning those glasses did fall off. Miss Dessa slipped down the steps when she came out to greet us. "You wait here. I'll go get Momma," I said to Baby Sister. Momma brought the doctor.

"You keep off that sore foot for awhile," the doctor told Miss Dessa.

"We'll stay here and take care of her," I said. "We'll stay at Miss Dessa's house all day and all night until she's better."

Momma told us to be good. She said she'd be back at suppertime to check on us.

"Let's fix Miss Dessa's glasses so they won't fall off again," I suggested. "How about red yarn?"

"Miss Dessa likes blue," Baby Sister replied, as she rummaged through the yarn bag. So we tied blue yarn on Miss Dessa's glasses and she never had to worry about them falling off again.

"There's coffee and biscuits on the stove," Miss Dessa said. Coffee always simmered on the stove and buttered biscuits sat in the warmer oven. Even in summer, a low fire smoldered in the firebox.

"Don't tell Momma about the coffee," I said to Baby Sister. Even though Miss Dessa put plenty of milk and sugar in it, I knew Momma wouldn't like young'uns drinking coffee.

Miss Dessa sat in her rocker and sewed quilt pieces together.
"Sit beside me, Girl, and I'll show you," she said to me. Baby
Sister was too little to use a needle. When she started pouting
at being left out, Miss Dessa gave her a basket of thread.

"Pick out some colors for us," she said.

Miss Dessa made quilts on a frame that hung from the ceil-
ing. Together we worked on a special quilt for her daughter
who lived in New York City.

In the back room there was an old trunk. In that trunk were old wide-tailed dresses and smushed-down hats.

"We're all dressed up, Baby Sister, like grand ladies!" We sashayed about in high-heeled shoes, smiling at ourselves in the mirror. We loved pulling things out of that trunk and making a mess in the back room.

At lunchtime Baby Sister and I took a tray of biscuits and jam to Miss Dessa. We played outside, while she rested on the porch.

Chinaberries were scattered all about the yard. The berries made perfect pellets for our homemade blowguns.

"I'm gonna get you," I told Baby Sister. My berry blew right past her. She ducked and curved and ran.

Then she blew and yelled, "Gotcha!"

Miss Dessa laughed at us, while Lazy Dog snoozed by her side.

"Let's pick flowers for Miss Dessa," Baby Sister whispered. We ran to the flower garden to get black-eyed Susans and deep-red roses. We gathered yellow sunflowers and Queen Anne's lace. We picked hollyhocks and ruffled heads of hydrangea.

"They smell so good," I said. "Let's sneak them inside to the kitchen table. Won't Miss Dessa be surprised?"

An old tire dangled on a frayed rope from an oak tree.
"Push me!" Baby Sister said, climbing into the tire. I
pushed hard and the rope broke, dumping her into the dirt.

"You pushed too hard," she cried, sniffling. Baby Sister ran and hid her face in Miss Dessa's lap.

"She didn't mean to hurt you, Child," Miss Dessa said. She hugged Baby Sister close.

"How about the three of us play Zudie-O," Miss Dessa suggested, reaching for my hands. We moved our arms back and forth to the rhythm as we sang:

Let's go zudie-o, zudie-o, zudie-o,
let's go zudie-o all night long.

Baby Sister strutted and danced her way between us while we clapped and sang:

Strut Miss Sally, Sally, Sally,
strut Miss Sally, all night long.
Walking through the valley, valley, valley,
walking through the valley all night long.
Here comes another one, another one,
* another one,*
just like the other one, all night long.

"Now, how about you girls go play some more," Miss Dessa said. "You two don't need to be fretting over me." I told Baby Sister to start counting while I went to hide.

"One, two, three," she counted.

"Don't you peek. Keep your eyes shut tight." I ran behind the house. But then I changed my mind and hid behind the big tree down the hill.

Suddenly, Lazy Dog started barking! "Quiet, Lazy Dog! Baby Sister will find me for sure."

But Lazy Dog kept barking and ran to the house. Miss Dessa was up and walking.

"Miss Dessa!" I yelled, running up the hill.

"I'm fine, Child. Just testing my foot."

Baby Sister and I helped Miss Dessa to her rocker and suggested she close her eyes and rest some more.

We tip-toed off to pick an afternoon snack of peaches and plums. Juice ran between our fingers and down our arms, sticky and sweet and good.

"Pick some for Miss Dessa," I said. "We'll save some for Momma, too." Later on, we surprised her when she and Poppa dropped off supper for all of us.

At day's end, we helped Miss Dessa get ready for bed. We unpinned her hair, letting it fall down her back.

"Come on, Baby Sister. Let's comb it and brush it and plait it."

Miss Dessa was patient with us. She talked while we combed her hair.

"It gets lonely here sometimes," she said. "You girls make me wish my daughter and her family lived closer. It does my heart good to have young'uns playing and running in the yard."

Miss Dessa pulled Baby Sister onto her lap. "I can't complain though," she said. "I have the best neighbors in the world, I have Lazy Dog to keep me company, and you girls come to see me all the time." Baby Sister and I hugged Miss Dessa tight.

"Let's read Miss Dessa a bedtime story," Baby Sister said. I found an old book of fairy tales and read aloud. Miss Dessa snuggled under the patch-work coverlet, her eyelids drooping and her breathing soft. I carefully laid Miss Dessa's glasses on the dresser and Baby Sister tucked her in.

"Now, we'll straighten up this house and get ourselves ready for bed," I said. We put the grown-up dresses back in the trunk. Set out supper for Lazy Dog. Stored our blow-guns back under the porch.

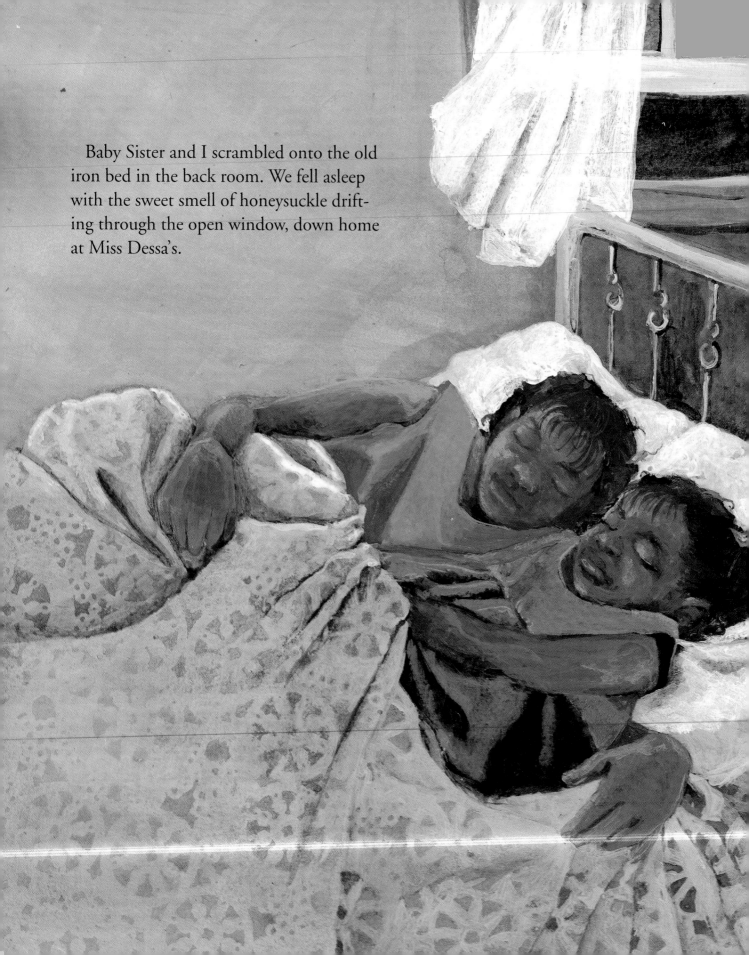

Baby Sister and I scrambled onto the old iron bed in the back room. We fell asleep with the sweet smell of honeysuckle drifting through the open window, down home at Miss Dessa's.